Rupert's Tales: Friendship is Magick, too

Seeing through the Storm

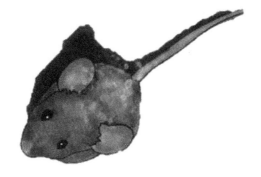

Written by Kyrja
Illustrated by Lesli Pringle-Burke

ISBN: 978-1-64606-717-6

Author's Dedication

With gratitude for those who do better when they learn better.

Illustrator's Dedication

These stories are gratefully dedicated to my children Scott, Ryan, Linzi, Briana & Victor whom always inspire me to live my truth and never give up. My mother Jeanne, who taught me the magic of imagination and remembering to keep the child in me alive. To all of the children who ever felt different. And last but not least to Twiggy & Snooki my faithful companions who were by my side every moment while creating every illustration in these pages. Without them I would have finished them sooner!

Rupert the rabbit was running and hopping through the deep snow.
He wanted to go faster, but instead went a little slow.

His friend, Melvin the mouse, was with him, and he was running too,
Melvin was small, so going slower was the right thing to do.

Still, Rupert was cold and wet, and the wind was really blowing.
There was a barn just up ahead, and that's where they were going.

He had seen these kinds of things before, maybe a time or two,
But barns and the things inside of them, for Rupert, were brand new.

For days now the winter wind had been strong and so bitter cold,
So, even with his thick, warm fur, this weather was getting old.

Melvin said he knew a of place that was safe and would be warm,
And so here they were, somewhere to get out of the awful storm.

The barn was a building that looked something like a people house.
It didn't look like a good place for a rabbit and a mouse.

But Rupert knew Melvin, and he knew he could trust his good friend,
And so he squeezed hard through a small crack in the wall, in the end.

He saw right away this was not like a people house at all.
Instead of rooms, there were piles of hay and a row of stalls.

He was glad to be out of the wind and the cold of the storm,
And was thankful Melvin knew someplace that was both safe and warm.

He would have liked it even better if there had been more light.
But with his keen eyes and good long ears, he knew they'd be all right.

They were not alone here; that was something he could safely say.
He could hear things moving in the shadows not too far away.

"You don't have to worry," Melvin told him, "I've been here before."
"If the people come inside, you can hide right behind that door."

He had lived in a people house, and did not want to return.
That he didn't like cages hadn't taken him long to learn.

Another thing he didn't like was what he could see right now.
Coming right towards them was trouble he would have to fix somehow.

Rupert often liked meeting new friends and getting to know them too,
But he didn't think that was what the big, black rats would want to do.

They looked mean and mad, and just looking at them gave him a fright.
But it was hard to see more than tails and eyes in this dark light

There were five of them on their way across the barn's wide, wood floor,
And something was behind that door, so there might be even more!

Rupert looked at Melvin to see what his friend might be thinking,
He found Melvin was looking straight up, without even blinking.

Looking up, Rupert cried out then, just as scared as he could be.
When he saw wings overhead, he yelled "Oh no! Please don't eat me!"

But the owl that was coming kept going, and flew right on past,
He scattered the rats every which way; it happened very fast.

The owl chased the rats this way and that, and all over the place!
It was funny, Rupert thought to himself, to watch such a chase.

He was glad to see, though, that the owl wasn't hurting the rats.
He was just chasing them until they hid in the wood floor slats.

"Hey! That wasn't very nice!" he heard one of the rats call out.
"We never did anything to you!" he heard another shout.

Rupert stood quite still as the owl landed on the floor close by.
He no longer felt so scared, although he couldn't say just why.

He almost changed his mind though, when the owl turned his head around,
His eyes both flew open wide, and he made a loud gasping sound.

"You only have one eye!" he shouted out, taken by surprise,
"Rupert! That's not nice," Melvin scolded, "nor is it very wise."

"Our friend, the owl here, was trying to help us, I'm sure you know."
"I think an apology," Melvin frowned, "is something you owe."

"That's all right," the owl sighed sadly, "although I'm sorry to say,"
"It happens all the time, but I just never know what to say."

"I'm sorry," he told the owl. "My name is Rupert, by the way."
"But what do you mean?" he asked, "that you don't know what you should say?"

"What I don't understand," the owl said, "and I just cannot see,"
"Is why everyone has to say something about it to me."

"Do you really think I don't know, or that I don't have a clue,"
"That I look very different than the way the rest of you do?

"Oh," Rupert said, feeling really quite small. "I see better now."
"Why does it matter," Melvin asked, "what he looks like anyhow?

"Hey! That's not fair!" they heard a voice call out from across the way,
"Yeah, you did the very same thing, Odan, in just the same way!"

"Who?" asked the owl. "Tell me how did I do such an awful thing?"
"I wouldn't use words to hurt others, I know how much they sting!"

"Maybe not with words," said one rat, "but you chased us all away,"
Another said, "Before you even heard what we had to say!"

"You thought we would hurt them," said a third rat, "Come on, tell us true."
"You treated us just exactly like Rupert there, treated you."

Rupert watched as Odan cocked his head and blinked his one good eye.
"No," he said, "That's not quite true, but it was a very good try."

"I've watched you rats for four long days and all through the long, dark nights."
"You steal all the food, spill the water, and get in many fights."

"So you might better understand, here's another thing that's true, "
"Each of us is very different, but we are just "rats" to you."

"You don't even know our names," the rat said, "though we all know yours."
"When you know someone's name, then they're not so easy to ignore."

"You're no longer strangers," said another, "like you were before."
"It's a beginning," said a third, "and can sometimes lead to more."

"But, like Rudy here, you won't always like everyone you meet,"
A small rat said, "I don't like him because he has stinky feet!"

Rupert laughed when Rudy playfully smacked the other rat's ear,
But he knew there was an important lesson to be learned here.

"Odan isn't the only one who thought you might bring us harm,"
"I admit," Rupert said, "when we arrived I was quite alarmed!"

"All I could see was bright eyes, long tails, and a lot of sharp teeth."
"I didn't stop to think about who you might be underneath."

"And you, Odan," Rupert went on, "scared me right out of my mind!"
"When I first saw you, I didn't think you'd be friendly and kind."

"He's not!" one of the rats yelled. "He thinks we're all nothing but bad."
"Sometimes" another said softly, "that makes me feel kind of sad."

"But you take all the food!" Odan said, "and that's not nice at all!"
"You spill, you fight, and have made a mess in every single stall."

"So tell me then, rat," Odan said, leaning close to make his point,
"With all of this, how can I help but to have a bad viewpoint?"

"My name is Ryan," said the rat, "What about the things you steal?"
"Some corn is missing from the place we've put the things for our meals."

"I'm Roger," said another. "I don't like how you look at me."
"You're always frowning, so I often wonder just what you see."

"Yes," agreed Rudy, "why don't you try to have some fun with us?"
"Maybe then you wouldn't be so grumpy and make such a fuss."

"I'm Rollin," said rat number four. "You may only have one eye,"
 "We're afraid you'll grab and eat us, when you fly down from the sky."

They all turned to the last rat, to see what he would have to say.
"Well," said Odan, "come on, out with it, we haven't got all day."

"Rudy, Ryan, Roger, and Rollin. Does your name start with "R" too?"
"No," the small rat said softly, "my name is Francis. How do you do?"

That's when they heard a burst of laughter come from behind the door.
A long nose peeked slowly out, two small eyes, and then something more.

"It's a weasel!" called out Roger. "No," said Ryan, "he's a cat!"
"No," said the stranger, "I'm not any of those you silly rats."

"I'm a ferret, my name is Flynn, and I live in the people house."
"Now we all have met each other, except for you," he said, "the mouse."

Rupert could tell Melvin didn't like something about this Flynn,
It was in his eyes, and in the way he raised his little chin.

"Melvin the mouse," he said, "and now I have a question for you,"
"Do you know where the missing corn is?" he asked. "I think you do."

Odan's head turned quickly, and all the rats looked right at Flynn too.
Rupert watched closely, wondering just what the ferret would do.

Everyone else thought the other had been stealing all along,
But now it looked like, maybe, each of them had really been wrong.

"You live in the people house," Rupert said, "so why are you here?"
"That is a story I bet that all of us would like to hear."

Rupert saw Melvin smile at him, and felt all warm inside.
It made him feel like he was smart, and even a little wise.

Flynn looked all around, at all five rats, and at the angry owl,
He looked up and down, looked at Melvin, and then the ferret scowled.

19

"I was curious, you see," he said. "The people went away."
"I was bored, all alone, and I really just wanted to play."

"I found a window that was open to let in some fresh air,"
"The window closed when I jumped out, but I didn't really care."

"At least," Flynn smiled, "Until I saw all the snow on the ground."
Rupert was glad the rats all smiled; they were coming around.

"But why did you steal the food?" Odan frowned. "That was very bad."
"If you would have asked," Rollin said, "We would have shared what we had."

"I think," said Rupert, "that is one answer, we already know."
"All of here have a habit that might be wise to outgrow."

Melvin smiled at him again, so Rupert kept on going.
"If we're scared of each other, our list of friends will stop growing."

"You're right my furry friend," said Odan, "though I'm surprised to say,"
"I never really looked at friendship, before, in quite that way."

"I still don't like the way Rudy's feet smell," said Francis with a wink
 "But even when we don't like someone, we can get along, I think."

Rupert smiled, wondering if the storm would last for many days.
Maybe there would be time for all of them to start to mend their ways.

About the Author

Kyrja celebrates Sabbats, moon phases and other magickal gatherings with Friends of Rupert and performs "Rupert's Tales and Tunes" at festivals and other events. She continues to work on future tales featuring Rupert and his friends, as well as fantasy-genre fiction novels. She has been the captain of an Adopt-A-Road crew for more than nine years, helping to take care of Mother Earth. Kyrja also likes to write and sing children's songs so may burst suddenly into song at any given moment.

About the Illustrator

Lesli Pringle-Burke is an artist that enjoys bringing bright characters to life through her Magical Realism style of painting. She currently resides in Saint Petersburg Florida where she continues painting and teaching out of her downtown home studio. Her work has been featured in many magazines and can be found hanging in shops and galleries in Downtown Saint Petersburg, and on the walls of private collections all over the world.

Other Rupert's Tales titles by the Author

- Rupert's Tales: Wheel of the Year—Beltane, Litha, Lammas and Mabon
- Rupert's Tales: Wheel of the Year—Samhain, Yule, Imbolc, and Mabon
- Rupert's Tales: The Wheel of the Year Activity Book
- Rupert's Tales: Rupert Helps Clean Up
- Rupert's Tales: A Book of Bedtime Stories
- Rupert's Tales: Learning Magick
- Rupert's Tales: Making More Magick
- Rupert's Tales: The Nature of Elements
- Rupert's Tales: What's in a Name?

CPSIA information can be obtained
at www.ICGtesting.com
Printed in the USA
BVHW010310090919
557662BV00014B/281/P

9 781646 067176